This Journal is the Property of:

Sean Campden

Please don't forget to write a review on Amazon

Thank you

Any Kid U.S.A

TELLING STORIES   And   NAMING NAMES

AUTHOR: A. SWIFT

Any Kid U.S.A

TELLING AND STORIES

NAMING NAMES

If my little brother Ben got caught doing something wrong, nothing would have happened to him. He never gets into trouble. His "day job" is being a brat, and he's good at it too.

...GOT SO MUCH IT'S WAS LIKE A TOY STORE TOYS, VIDEO GADGETS THAN NOW HE'S EVEN GOT A TON OF 3D GAMES, WE FORGOT ALL ABOUT SLAPPY

BY A. SWIFT

ILLUSTRATED BY JAMES VANN AND RONALDO FLORENDO

To my Mom who encouraged me
in everything I did.

Thursday, August 22

Mom bought me this DIARY last Christmas.
Okay, that's the last time I'll call it a diary.
I like to say it's my JOURNAL. Journal sounds a
lot better. I NEVER used it because I never
had anything to write about— until now.
I had this COOL dream last night, so I decided
to write about it. In the dream, a ninja guy kept
calling me names. That didn't bother me, but
when he asked if my "mommy" dressed me, I
couldn't take it anymore.

It was time he took a ride on the "pain-train."
Nobody comes into MY dream and talks to me
like that. I told him, "If you ever see me
wrestling a racoon don't help me, help the
racoon." He laughed at me. He reminded me of
this character in the video game *The
Grandmaster's Strike*. I beat that guy up all the
time.

I made two moves and before he knew it, he
was on the ground begging me to let him up. I
didn't think he'd go down THAT easy.

I decided to let him go. He was crying like a
BABY. It was kind of embarrassing.

My teacher at school said, "Important people have journals to write down all the important stuff that happens to them in life." I wanna be important too.

That's why I have this journal. I'm not sure if having dreams of video game characters is the kind of junk important people write in their journals, but that's what I'm writing in mine.

My sister, Starr doesn't like me calling this my journal. She wants me to call it a diary.
She LIKES to aggravate me on purpose.

Starr HAS a diary, and it's filled with a whole bunch of dumb stuff. I know because I read it. It was just sitting on her bed. I couldn't help myself. I read about ten pages before Starr came into the room and caught me. She was SOOO MAD. And she didn't waste any time telling Mom.

I wish I could say reading her diary was worth the punishment, but it wasn't. All she writes about is going to the movies, putting on make-up, going to the mall and meeting boys. It was the most BORING thing I ever read.

I can't believe I got into trouble for that. If my little brother Ben got caught doing something like that, nothing would have happened to him. He never gets into trouble. His "day job" is being a brat, and he's good at it too.

If he doesn't get his way, he'll either throw a tantrum or do something mean. Once he asked me to get him a cookie from the kitchen. When I told him I wouldn't do it, he went to school the next day and told all of his friends about it.

And he didn't just TELL them, he gave a speech, and called it, "My ROTTEN Big Brother Sean." He had pictures of the family and everything. In the speech, he said Mom and Dad were great to him, and that he had an awesome big sister named Starr. But once he got to me, he got really mean. He passed around a book so the kids could read about ALL the times I wasn't nice to him.

I'm still trying to figure out how he was able to make a book. In the book, he said I was the lowest of the low and MEANEST of the mean. I told him I wanted us to be friends again, and that he could have one of MY cookies in the jar on top of the fridge. Then I went and told Mom he was eating cookies before dinner. Yeah, that was kind of mean, but it was fun.

Friday, August 23th

Tomorrow's a big day. We're moving to a new town, and into a bigger house. My best friend Devin still doesn't believe it. He thinks I'm kidding around.

One thing I'm worried about is how Devin and the rest of these people in the neighborhood are going to get along without me. Who's going to tell Mrs. Walerbee her dog is missing?

Who's going to help Devin make fun of
Marcell when she comes home from work?

She always makes it so EASY for us to make fun of her. It doesn't take much work at all.

Mom wanted ME to tell Ben to come inside and start packing. When I told him, he said I had to WAIT a minute because he was saying goodbye to his friends.

When he said "friends", he didn't mean people. He meant the ants, beetles and worms in the backyard. At first, he was saying goodbye to them one at a time. Goodbye ant. So long worm.

I thought that was crazy, but then it got even CRAZIER. He said, he wouldn't leave without them, and started grabbing BUGS off the ground, and sticking them in his pocket.

Mom's not going to like this, but at least I won't get in trouble for this one. This is all on him.

Saturday, August 24th

It's moving day. The moving guys got here super early. And I was in bed half asleep NOT wanting to get up. Mom or Dad could have tried to wake me, but instead they sent their "secret weapon," my sister Starr.

Why Starr? Because she's GOOD at it! I was
surprised that she didn't try her USUAL bang on
my door yelling "IT'S TIME TO GET UP" thing.
Instead she did something NEW. She turned on
the BIG hallway light.

It's the brightest light in the house. Then she
opened my door and walked away. I thought I'd

go blind with that light shining in my face, so I had to get up.

I wonder who's teaching her this stuff. To be honest, I would have gotten up anyway.

Those moving guys were making so much noise I couldn't go back to sleep.

What does a kid have to do to get some rest around here? It's really kind of dumb that people have to get up so early to do work.

If I were king of the WORLD, I'd make a bunch of rules so we could ALL sleep late.

KING SEAN'S RULES

Rule #1: Nobody will be allowed to get up
early to do anything.
No Bakers, No School Teachers and
Especially No Moving Men!

Rule #2: If you have something important
to do in the morning, SEE RULE #1

Rule #3: All you "early morning animals"
like
The Hen:
lay your eggs in the afternoon.
The Rooster:
I hear your cock-a doodle do, I say
cock-a-doodle DON'T!

The "Early Bird":
You like to catch the worm?
Why don't you eat something else.

Worms are yucky.

KING SEAN HAS SPOKEN!

I'm not sure if those birds would be able to read my rules. I might have to talk to them face to...beak.

I bet as soon as I did all that, Mom and Dad would overrule me. They'd tell everyone to start working early again, just so the moving men could come to the house before the sun comes up. Parents have WAY too much power.

THREE moving guys were supposed to come to the house this morning, but only TWO showed.

I guess the third guy couldn't get up that early.
Guy number three is all right in my book.

They told Dad not to worry, and that the two of
them could handle it themselves. At first, I
thought these guys were nuts! There's no way
just two people could move all our stuff.

Boy, was I wrong! Those two guys really know
how to work. They only stopped once, and that
was to eat lunch. I never saw two guys do so
much so fast.

I wish me and Ben could work together like that. He's lazy, and he gets bored too quickly. After about three minutes, he'd start to complain.

What's worse, I found out from Dad that those two guys were brothers. They must have taken a how-to-work-really-hard-with-your-brother class. Me and Ben would definitely have to take that class.

Sunday, August 25th

It took almost all day, but we finally have
everything in the new house. I still can't believe
two guys did all that work. Mom wasn't totally
happy; she found a crack in her coffee
table— and went berserk.

She ran outside to find the moving men.
When she saw the biggest of the two guys,
she walked right up to him and let him have it.

I've only seen Mom angry like that one other time. It was when I locked her keys in the car with Starr's sweet-sixteen birthday cake in the front seat. It had to be one hundred degrees out that day. The cake never made it home, but the car smelled AWESOME for a month.

Dad went outside to calm things down.
The moving guy tried to talk his way out of it
but, she wasn't having it.

The moving guy finally gave in and said he'd pay
for the table which made Mom calm down.

While the guys were packing up to leave, Dad
gave the big guy a TIP for the good job they
did. I was glad because Mom really read that
guy the riot act. He looked a little down, so I
think the tip helped to cheer him up.

As soon as they drove off, Dad said he was taking us all out for dinner. After all that, Mom looked like she could use a night out.

Mom said we could pick the place because all she wanted was a salad. At first, we all couldn't agree on where to go. Starr wanted tacos, and Ben wanted candy— as usual. Dad didn't know what he wanted. And just before I could say what I wanted Ben started yelling BURGER CERR-GA, BURGER CERR-GA!!!

Nobody knew what he was trying to say, not even me, and I always understand him.

And then I SAW what he was talking about. It was Burger Circus. The best burger place in the whole wide world, and Ben spotted it first.

I couldn't believe it. A real-life Burger Circus. The only time I ever actually saw one was on a TV commercial. Now we live right down the street from one. The great thing was, I already knew the whole menu from the commercial.

They had salads for Mom and a bunch of
different sandwiches that Dad would like.
Ben and me like almost everything on the
menu, so it was the perfect place for all of us
to eat. But then I remembered Starr. I almost
forgot about her. She was sitting there with her
arms crossed, NOT looking happy.

Then she said what I expected her to say: "I
don't want to go to Burger Circus." Ben heard
that and got woozy like he was going to pass
out. I got a little dizzy myself. I couldn't let
Starr stop us from going to Burger Circus. I
thought about getting out of the car and making

a mad dash for the restaurant, but I didn't have to. Mom straightened everything out.

She thought Starr's clown excuse was so wacky that she just laughed. Then she got out of the car to go inside the restaurant.

The place was awesome inside! They made you feel like you were actually at the circus.

The place had everything— animals too, but they were FAKE. It's probably better that way. Animals eat too much. They'd eat their food and then come after yours.

When the waitress came over to take our order, everyone knew what they wanted except for Dad.

The waitress asked him if he'd like to try the "Big Top Burger Challenge." He didn't know what that was and neither did the rest of us. So, she pointed to the poster on the wall.

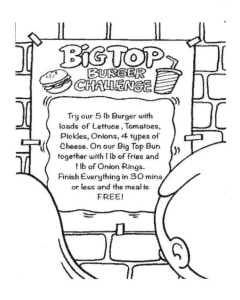

It turned out to be a burger eating contest. I thought Dad should definitely try it.

Mom's always telling him not to eat so much. If he puts himself in the contest, he can eat as much as he wants. After reading the poster, Dad asked the waitress a few questions.

She told him that only TWO guys were able to eat ALL of the Big Top Burger meal. When he heard that, his face SANK.

I didn't think he'd put himself in the contest after hearing that. Then something GREAT happened.

The waitress told him he had to sit at a special "eating contest" table. Then, minutes later, she showed up with the biggest cheeseburger I've ever seen in my life.

He only had thirty minutes to finish the whole thing. After she sat the burger down, she started the contest.

Dad didn't waste any time. He was STUFFING food in his mouth with both hands. It was going in faster than he could chew it.

He finished his fries first, then the onion rings. He was doing great.

He had plenty of time to finish the big burger. Dad started to draw a crowd. They were really cheering him on.

More time went by, and he only had a small piece of cheeseburger left to finish. But he didn't look like he could eat another bite.

There were only a few seconds left. The CROWD counted down ten, nine, eight, seven, six, five... Dad grabbed the last piece of food on his plate and stuffed it in his mouth right before time ran out. The crowd went wild!

I thought they would pick him up and carry him out of the restaurant on their shoulders.

That wouldn't have been a good idea. Dad wasn't looking so good. I guess I wouldn't either if I had a pile of cheeseburger, fries and onion rings floating around in MY stomach. I thought the fact that he ate all that food was pretty amazing.

I couldn't wait to see Dad's picture up on the wall with those other big top burger guys.

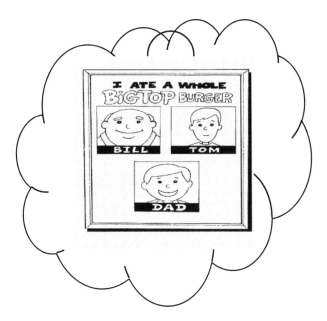

But then A REALLY crumby thing happened.
The waitress came over to clear Dad's tray and
found an onion ring underneath the table.

33

After the waitress FOUND that onion ring, she had to tell Dad he didn't win. The news made him sick to his stomach. I'm not kidding.

Right after she told him that, he started moaning, groaning and rubbing his stomach.

Luckily, it didn't last long, I went over to check on him and he was already looking and sounding better.

I was pretty proud of Dad. Who cares if he didn't win? He wasn't going to let some DUMB contest bring him down.

But then his whole mood changed when the waitress brought over the BILL for the Big Top Burger meal. I guess he forgot what the poster said. *"Finish EVERYTHING, and the meal is free."* All that food must have cost a fortune. I'm sure it did. He took one look at that BILL, grabbed his stomach, and the moaning and groaning started all over again.

Even though Dad didn't have the best time, I thought Burger Circus was pretty cool. On the way out of the restaurant, I saw that they were having

a HOTDOG eating contest next week. I thought
that would be perfect for Dad!

Monday, August 26th

I can't believe school is next week already.
Mom is supposed to register me for middle
school tomorrow. She said the school is so
close to the house that I can walk. That means
I don't have to ride the school bus.

That's a good thing. There's nothing wrong with the school bus, but sometimes me and school buses don't mix.

Like the time Ralphie Steppen missed his bus and had to ride OURS home. Ralphie's the class clown, but sometimes he's the "SCHOOL BUS clown" too. Taking our bus meant he had a whole NEW crowd of kids that never saw him do his Ralphie dance. He was in a few of my classes, so any time we had a substitute teacher, it was dancing time for Ralphie.

Sometimes he added something new. This day, he tried to add a little spin move. I don't think he knew he was going to do it until he did it. And it got big laughs.

Then, he tried a second spin, and that got even BIGGER laughs. Because in the middle of that second spin his pants dropped to the floor.

Everybody was laughing, even the bus driver.
After that, things got out of control. Kids were
standing on the seats pointing at Ralphie. School
supplies were flying around the bus. Kids were
falling on the school bus floor, laughing.

The bus driver tried to calm things down, but no
one could hear him. Somebody was shooting
spitballs, and I almost got hit. I was lucky.
Charlie Gramner wasn't so lucky. He got shot
with a spitball while his mouth was wide open.

Everybody STOPPED laughing at Ralphie's pants and started laughing at Charlie with the BIG spit ball in his mouth. I jumped out of my seat because I was in the line of fire.

Just as I did, the bus came to a stop. Everyone jerked forward including me, and my head hit the seat in front of me. I walked home from the bus stop with a lump on my head.

As soon as I got home, Mom saw the lump and asked a million questions to find out how it got there. She said the bus driver needs to do a better job supervising the kids on the bus.

I don't blame the bus driver; I blame Ralphie and his BAD dancing.

Tuesday, August 27th

Today, Mom registered me for school. It turns out she knew the administration lady from somewhere, and they were talking non-stop.

I tried giving her one of MY "I want to go home faces," but they were so busy talking, she never saw it. I thought they were going to talk forever and ever. Okay, I'm exaggerating a little.

I knew they'd have to stop talking at some point. Starr always tells me I exaggerate. She's been saying that for a while now, ever since the time we got stuck on the Ferris wheel.

I was seven years old. Starr was pretty young too. I was afraid to get on the Ferris wheel to begin with. As soon as the ride started moving, I heard something go CLICK, CLANK and the Ferris wheel stopped.

We were up in the air, STUCK on an amusement park ride, not knowing if we were ever getting off. Mom and Dad seemed fine with the whole thing. Not me. I was calling for help!

It seemed like nobody wanted to help. People
didn't even look up. I don't know if they thought
we were supposed to climb out of that
contraption or what.

I thought Mom and Dad were WAY too calm.
That's why nobody was paying attention to us.
I wasn't going to make the same mistake.

Nobody was taking the situation seriously enough so, I decided to ratchet up "THE CRAZY." I yelled my head off until FINALLY someone came over and got us out of that thing.

I don't care what Starr says about me exaggerating; Mom and that lady were talking for a really long time.

It went on for a bit longer, and then they just stopped talking. I guess they ran out of stuff to talk about, so we were able to leave. When we got home, there were these strangers standing in the living room talking to Dad.

THESE ARE OUR NEW NEIGHBORS, THE PATTONGALE'S AND THEIR DAUGHTER JANET.

They seemed like nice people, but that girl Janet, I wasn't too sure about. She was staring at me and not saying anything. Maybe she wanted to say something, and forgot what she was going to say. Maybe it was the NEW shirt I was wearing. She probably liked the way it looked on me. Maybe she liked ME. She was probably saying to herself "He's really cute." Yeah, that had to be what she was thinking.

Dad came over to us and said he had great news. Usually, when Dad says he's got great news, it's never great news. And like always, it wasn't. In fact, it was the worst news possible.

YOU TWO WILL BE WALKING TO SCHOOL TOGETHER.

No offense against her. She seems like an okay person, but I was planning on walking to school by myself.

If girls at school see me with her, they'll think I already have a girlfriend, and they won't want to talk to me. As soon as the Pattongale's left to go home, I talked to Mom and Dad.

I tried to explain to them that I need to look like a **SINGLE** guy when I go to school. Mom said she wanted me to concentrate on school and nothing else. Then she said if anything, the girls will like me more if they saw me with Janet.

That made no sense to me at all.

Why would a girl like you MORE if she saw you with another girl? I guess that only makes sense to adults. It's like these ADULTS have a different kind of brain, or something.

Wednesday, August 28th

This kid named Dino Gramney was riding his bike up and down my street today. He's the worse bicycle rider I ever saw. Every time he tried to do some kind of bike trick, he'd crash into something.

When he crashed into the garbage can, I went over to help him off the ground, and to make sure he didn't need any band-aids. He seemed like a cool kid, and his bike was pretty cool too.

He's got the kind of bike I've ALWAYS wanted. It's not too big, it has a small seat, and it's got HAND BRAKES! I've never had a bike with hand brakes before. My birthday is in a couple of weeks. The only thing I told Mom and Dad I wanted was a book called the "World's Creepiest People". I'm going to tell them I want

a new bike too, just like Dino's. Since Mom was
on her way home, I tried to get Dino to hang
around so she could see it, but he wouldn't do it.

YOU CAN'T
WAIT FIVE
MINUTES?

NOPE.
I HAVE
HOMEWORK
TO FINISH.

I thought he was joking about the homework,
because we're still on our summer break, but he
wasn't. He then rattled off a bunch of other
stuff his Mom makes him do.

Like he can only stay outside an HOUR on
school days. He can't play video games on

school days either. He's not allowed to have a
TV in his room. And a whole bunch of other
stuff I can't remember.

Geez, and I thought my Mom and Dad were
strict. Dino tried to do one last bike trick before
he went home. It didn't turn out so good.

Thursday, August 29th

Today, I told Mom about the bike I wanted for my birthday.

I found a picture of the bike I want on the internet, and printed it out to show her.

She took one look at it and said, "You're not ready for a bike like that." She said, "That's a BIG KID'S bike, and you're not a big kid yet." I had to think of a way to show her I was a big kid really quick.

Mom saw I wasn't giving up on the idea, so she told me the REAL reason she didn't think I was ready for the bike. She said that when she was my age, she was riding her friend's bike with

HAND BRAKES. She thought she was going a little too fast, so she squeezed really hard on one of the brakes and went flying off the bike. She only had a few bruises from the fall, but her Mom really got on her case.

AHHHH!!

If I had that bike, I don't think that would've happened to me, but I didn't tell Mom that. After her story, she said, "No hand brakes. You're getting a bike with PEDAL brakes." I just shook my head okay, and went into my room, but I still wasn't giving up. Sometimes after Mom thinks about stuff, she changes her mind.

So, I was hoping if I wait a while and ask her again, she'll say YES to the bike I want.

I waited an hour and asked again. I guess she needed more time because she was still saying no. So, I waited another hour and tried again, and she said, "No" again.

I thought about pleading my case to Dad, but he was so busy playing with the remote, I don't think he even knew I was in the room.

He'd probably agree with Mom anyway.
They agree on mostly everything. And if they
don't agree on something, she gives Dad this
really mean look and like magic, all of a sudden,
he agrees with her.

Friday, August 30th

Mom says I need to be a "big kid" to get the
bike I want. The way I look at it, I'm already a

"big kid." She always says, "Ben's your LITTLE brother." That makes me his BIG brother. I figured if she sees me doing "big brother" stuff for Ben, she'll have to see that I'm big enough for that bike. It wasn't the greatest plan in the world, but it was a plan.

The only big brother thing I could think of to do was make him some breakfast. He's always hungry so it seemed like a good idea. The only MAJOR problem with the plan was BEN was in the plan. Anytime I try to get Ben's help, something goes wrong. Like the time I asked him to hold a chair steady for me.

BEN,... NO!!

But I tried anyway. I made the breakfast, woke him up, and sat him down. All I needed him to do was to tell Mom that I got him up early and made him a great breakfast. I didn't think that was too hard for him to do.

I thought not even Ben could mess that up but, I was wrong. First, he wanted to know why I woke him up so early. Then he tells me that I don't know how to make breakfast. Then he complained about the waffles I made him.

I knew as soon as Mom woke up, he'd tell her something I did that he didn't like, and ruin my plan. So, I had to bribe him.

I told him if he tells Mom I made him a great breakfast, and that I am the best BIG brother he ever had; I would give him a candy bar. It was a good idea, but Ben forgot everything I told him to say.

I didn't really expect that to work, and that's why I had a PLAN B. It was time to bring Dad into the picture. Dad has yard work to do today, and he doesn't like doing it.

Dad showed me how to cut the grass last year, so I knew I could do a pretty good job.

Once he sees the nice job I've done cutting the grass, all I have to do is tell him what bike I want, and then sit back and wait for him to convince Mom to get it for me.

The only problem was, I couldn't get the lawn mower out of the garage. There was a bunch of junk sitting right on top of it. I thought maybe Starr could help me move some of the stuff, but I couldn't get her off the phone.

I tried everything. I waved my arms up and down. Then I turned her TV volume way up, but nothing worked. Then something told me to throw my smelly socks at her. That might get her attention.

It got her attention alright. but the whole thing kind of backfired. One of the socks I threw landed right on her shoulder, and she lost it.

UGGGGH... HIS SMELLY SOCK IS ON ME!!!

Then it got worse. My other sock landed on her PILLOW. She screamed, picked up the pillow and stuffed it in the trash. I mean, c'mon, who does that? Then Mom came rushing in the room, wanting to know what was going on. After Starr told her what happened, I got sent out.

I had to stay in my room until dinner time, so I couldn't cut the grass for Dad. Another plan down the drain, thanks to Starr. Ben was no help to me either. Now I know why kids run off to join the circus.

Saturday, August 31st

When I woke up this morning, I heard noises outside my room. I thought it was Ben watching cartoons, but it was Mom doing her exercises in the living room.

I thought it was the perfect time to ask her about the bike again. And I was right.

In between the huffing and the puffing, she said, "You're getting your bike."

This is great! I'm finally getting a bike with hand brakes. Now I wish I didn't have to wait until my birthday. It would be great to get it before school starts. And it starts next week.

Dad already told that girl Janet Pattongale that I'd walk to school with her every morning. I wish there was a way I could get out of doing it.

The whole thing might feel weird, because we don't know each other that well. There is one GOOD thing that will come out of it.

At least I don't have to walk into that middle school for the first time by myself. I'm the new kid in school and kids you don't know look at you like you have two heads.

Sunday, September 1ˢᵗ

I walked over to Dino's house today and met this kid named Eddie Jasen.

He was there trying to talk Dino into going to his house to watch a video of Slappy Silver the comedian.

At first, Dino didn't want to go. He said he had school supplies to order.

Most people wait for the first day of school and then get a list of what to buy from the teacher. Dino's kind of a "maniac" about school, so he won't wait for school to start. He likes to make up the list himself.

Dino finished the list and then told Eddie he'd go to his house to watch the video. Eddie said he wanted me to watch it too. I didn't know exactly who Slappy was, but I've always heard

kids talking about him. I was okay with going—I
just had to stop off and let Mom know.

When we got to Eddie's house, he went looking
all over for the Slappy Silver DVD and couldn't
find it. Then he remembered his Dad was
watching it in the den. I couldn't understand why
his Dad would want to watch a kid's video. As
soon as Eddie turned it on and Slappy started
telling jokes, it all made sense. He was really
funny. That guy could make anybody laugh, and
he had us laughing— kind of loud.

That's probably what made Eddie's Mom come in the room.

As soon as she saw what we were watching, she turned the TV off. She said Slappy had a potty mouth and we should do something else. She told us to go to Eddie's room and play.
At first, I thought going to Eddie's room would be a bad thing, but it wasn't. He's got so much stuff in there, it was like being in a mini toy store. He's got more toys, video games and gadgets than anybody I know. He's even got a ton of virtual 3D games.

After playing video games he wanted to show us his treehouse. Who needs a treehouse? Maybe he just wanted to see if his parents would buy him one if he asked.

Eddie let me climb inside. It was comfortable, but I could never live in there. When I tried lying down, my feet were hanging out the front door.

Monday, September 2nd

Today was the first day of school. I was a little tired, so I thought it would be a good idea to start school next week, but Mom wasn't having it. She made me get up, and right before she left my room, said something that sounded like "Janet is a brown bear."

But I knew she couldn't have said that. It made no sense. I sat there thinking about it for a minute, and then it hit me. She didn't say, "Janet is a BROWN BEAR," she said, "Janet is DOWNSTAIRS." If Janet's downstairs, that means I'm LATE! I jumped out of bed and tried to run into the bathroom to wash up. But Ben's toy truck got in the way of my big toe.

It hurt like the H-E double hockey stick word I'm not supposed to say. When I got downstairs and saw Janet, I told her I was sorry for making us late for school. I thought she'd say we should RUN to school to make it there on time, but she didn't have to. Because we weren't late. She came to the house twenty minutes early, so we'd have plenty of time to walk to school,

I was a bit annoyed about Janet coming over so early. I rushed myself to get dressed and almost lost my big toe. At least the early start gave her a chance to tell me what I should know on my first day.

This walking to school with Janet thing worked out okay. It took us no time to get there, and we had a lot to talk about. Well, SHE had a lot to talk about. I mostly listened.

She can REALLY talk! I didn't even have to worry about any new GIRLS seeing us walk to school together. As soon as we got to the front entrance, she took off.

I wanted to ask her where my homeroom was, but she left so fast I never got the chance.

When I got inside the school, I looked around for somebody who could help me find where it was. Somebody that looked smart.
I looked for the smartest looking kid I could find.

It took a few minutes, but then I found this kid standing in the hall by himself.
He had such a BIG head I knew he had to know EVERYTHING. And I was right. He told me exactly where to go to find my first class.

That HEAD of his was jammed packed with information. I would have asked him to help me find ALL of my classes, but that would have taken too long. I was able to find the next few classes myself. Even the cafeteria.

I heard a bunch of kids talking about food so I followed them straight into the lunch room. Janet was already there. She called me over to sit with her and her two friends, Mia Gaffney and Kelly Kindale.

I knew Janet LIKES to talk. I found that out on our way to school this morning. But when she's sitting with her friends, the talking goes into overdrive.

They spent a lot of time talking about other kids at school. And they didn't have too many nice things to say about them, either.

They bad-mouthed this one, and talked trash about that one. It was sickening.

But it was only the first day of school.
I'm sure they don't do that every day.
After lunch, I had one more class. I thought I could find that class myself, too. Besides, the smart kid with the giant head was nowhere in sight.

When I got to the class, I was proud of myself. I found a seat and sat down, but something didn't feel right. Like maybe I was in the wrong class. I was. I was also in the WRONG seat.

I got out of there as fast as I could. Especially after he said that if I didn't get out of his seat, he'd sew my NOSE to my BUTT. I don't know if that's possible, but I wasn't sticking around to find out.

Wednesday, Sept 4th

I didn't write in my journal on Tuesday because NOTHING exciting happened.

And luckily, I didn't have any giant-sized
GOONS threatening me about where I was
sitting. I was wrong about Janet and her two
friends, Mia and Kelly. I thought they'd only
spend the FIRST day of school talking trash
about kids. NO, they do that EVERY day. At
least they don't say BAD things about
me—I hope.

Trash talking school kids all day can get boring
after a while. I'd rather talk about other stuff
like playing sports, riding bikes and playing video

games. The guys at the table close to ours were talking about ALL that stuff.

I thought if I stood close enough to their table, they'd SEE me and invite me over.

I felt kind of dumb just standing there, but it was better than sitting at the table with the girls.

Thursday, September 5th

It's a week before my birthday. That means next week, I'll be riding my new bike, with the fancy HAND BRAKES. I wanted Dino to know I was getting a bike like his, so I walked to his house to tell him about it. When I got there, he was sitting at his desk pretending to be working on something important. He said he was working on the "coolest thing ever," so I played along by trying to guess what he was doing.

First, I thought he might be making a list of his favorite super heroes. Then I thought he was working on new weapons for a video game. He wasn't working on any of that. After he told me what he was working on, I was disappointed.

85

At that point, I thought I should tell him what's "cool" and what's "not cool." Because that's what friends do. Getting a hundred on a test you didn't study for—that's cool! Getting a new puppy— that's cool! Finding money in a pair of pants you hardly wear— that's REALLY cool! Extra credit HOMEWORK you do when you get home from school, NOT so cool. I might have gone a little TOO far saying extra credit work wasn't cool, because he said I insulted him and then he tried to put me in a head lock.

I learned you can say whatever you want to Dino, but if you talk BAD about his extra credit work, he'll want to fight you. We heard Dino's Mom coming down the hall.

So, Dino ran behind his desk and sat down. I pretended to be interested in Dino's extra credit work. Two seconds later, she came in the room to tell us something.

The first thing I thought when she told us that was, "I don't have to sit with the girls at lunch anymore!" It will be cool to have Dino going to my school, but I wasn't sure if he wanted to go to a new school or not. So later on I asked him.

DO YOU WANT TO CHANGE SCHOOLS?

YEAH! I TOLD MY MOM I DIDN'T LIKE MY SCHOOL.

I thought he should know what he's in for. The teachers in my school don't fool around.
Tests all the time, homework every day. I didn't want to scare him, but he needed to know.

I should have known he'd be okay with TOO much homework. My school likes to give out extra credit homework too, but I knew not to say anything about that. All I have to do is bring up extra credit work and he'd be trying to head lock me again.

Wednesday, September 11th

Tomorrow is my birthday, which means TOMORROW I'll get my NEW bike. Since I'm getting a bike a lot like Dino's, I told him to bring his bike over so I could practice on it. He took FOREVER to show up to my house.

When he finally did, I gave him a new name. Slow-poke Dino I called him.

He told me he was at Eddie's for almost an hour, and now he's going home. I figured he was leaving because of the name I called him.

Thursday, September 12th

It's my birthday, and boy am I glad I didn't miss school today. This kid named Mike Ramo was walking back to his lunch table with his tray of food and accidentally tripped over Kathy Scotton's foot. His food went flying everywhere. And some of it landed on Kathy.

Mike went over to his table and sat down. Kathy grabbed her drink and walked over to Mike. Before he could say anything, he was taking a soda shower.

He didn't like that so, he started grabbing food anywhere he could get it, and threw it back at her. Then two teachers rushed over and broke it all up.

It was a good thing too. Other kids were getting hit with some of the food Mike and Kathy were throwing around. If those teachers hadn't stopped that, they would have had a good old fashion food fight on their hands.

That would have been something to see, and a pretty cool birthday present too. Mom and Dad brought home a birthday cake for me, and after dinner, I invited Dino and Eddie over to have cake and ice cream. I was glad they didn't waste a lot time coming over.

Anytime Ben sees cake and ice cream, he
rushes through dinner to get to it first.
He'll try and eat the whole thing if you let him.

While they ate cake, I was checking out one of
the gifts I asked for, The World's Creepiest
People book.

But I didn't see what I REALLY wanted and
that was my new bike. I asked Mom and Dad
about it— I thought maybe they just forgot to
buy it.

Then Dad said the people at the store needed extra time to put it together. That was okay with me because at least they didn't forget. But I couldn't understand why it was taking the bike store so long to put it together.

They had at least two weeks. Who's working on this thing anyway? That person must be the slowest worker of all time. Slow like a turtle. Maybe it's the half man, half turtle guy I saw in my Creepiest People book.

If that's who's putting bicycles together at the bike store, they should hire someone that could work a little faster. Maybe a half rabbit, half octopus guy?

Friday, September 13th

Today is Friday the 13th. It's definitely a day of bad luck for me. I'm on my way home from a hard day of middle school and, I see Mom and Dad outside with a brand-new bike. Since I've been asking for a new bike for over two weeks,

I had a feeling it was mine. There was only one problem— and it was MAJOR.

I rode around the block three times on my new bike. The bike is not bad, but it's not what I asked for. So, I wasn't TOTALLY happy.

I decided I was gonna show Mom and Dad that I was HAPPY because they did get me a NEW bike. So, I put on the happiest face I could muster up.

Saturday, September 14th

I wanted to try out my new bike with NO HAND BRAKES, at the bike trail. So, I called Dino to see if he wanted to go. He told me to meet him at Eddie's house. Chances are, Eddie will want to go, too. Eddie was trying out one of his new toy gadget things on one of the neighborhood kids.

I asked Eddie about the bike trail. He said he wanted to go, but he kept playing with his new toy. After about ten minutes Dino showed up, and we both waited for Eddie to finish. More time went by and he still wasn't ready.

We threatened to leave without him if he didn't let the kid down and get his bike.

He finally stopped to get his bike, but when he came back, we were a little upset at him.

Oh Boy, did we let him have it. We called him every BAD word we could think of— at least the ones we're allowed to say. Eddie still wanted to go with us even though he had no

bike. At that point, I didn't care. All those names we called him made me feel better. When we got to the bike trail, we took turns on the bikes, so Eddie could ride, too. That turned out to be a bad idea because Eddie was HOGGING all the riding time.

He started out on Dino's bike first. All Dino could do was stand there and watch while Eddie tooled around on his bike. Even when Dino tried to get his bike back by yelling, "Okay Eddie, it's MY turn!!" Eddie kept on riding.

Then, I tried yelling. "Okay Eddie, time to switch bikes. Give Dino his bike, and take mine." That didn't work either.

Finally, we saw Eddie heading our way. I thought for sure he was bringing Dino his bike.

At the last second, he stopped, turned the bike around, and headed back the other way. Eddie was acting like a real JERK. I knew if he ever brought Dino's bike back, he'd then want to ride my bike. And he'd keep my bike forever. We thought Eddie needed to be taught a lesson. So we decided to play a prank on him.

The plan was for me to hide. As soon as Dino got his bike back, he'd signal to me, and we'd take off riding.

We'd pretend to leave him stranded on the bike trail, then wait long enough for him to think that we really left him. Then we'd go back and get him. There's no way he'd try and walk back home it's too far. The plan was genius. I can't believe Dino helped me think of it. He's usually a moron when it comes to planning out stuff. When Eddie finally came back with Dino's bike, he asked where I was.

Eddie gave the bike back to Dino. Then Eddie stood there WAITING for me to show up. Dino had his bike, started riding, and then yelled out to me, "IT'S Prank-Time!!"

Eddie thought we were really leaving him, so he chased after us. That only lasted a little while; he got tired pretty fast and stopped running. We went around the corner to wait, and then Dino said he was bored. He thought we should go home and watch cartoons to kill time, but I knew that would have taken too long. So, we counted to one hundred— twice, and then rode back to get him. When we got to the place where we left him, he was gone. We rode around the trail, but couldn't find him anywhere. Then in the woods we heard screaming, and it sounded like Eddie. We raced to the spot where we heard the sound coming from, and we found him. He was running in circles screaming like a crazy person.

He didn't know that we saw him, and by the time we got to him he looked exhausted.

It took him a few minutes to catch his breath
before he could talk. When he COULD talk, he
asked if we were going to make fun of him for
running away from a rabbit.

I told him HECK YEAH!! He spent the next few
minutes trying to convince us that rabbits are
vicious and dangerous. I never heard of a rabbit
being dangerous.

Eddie said he once saw a rabbit and a tiger in a boxing match, and the rabbit knocked the tiger out cold.

I'm almost positive a rabbit can't lift eighty pounds. And just because you see a rabbit and a tiger fighting in a CARTOON that doesn't mean it really happened.

Monday, September 16th

I don't know why I got assigned home economics as one of my subjects at school. It's NOT one of my favorite classes. I know some people like to cook and sew— not me. All that stuff is hard work.

In my opinion, teaching kids to cook is a big waste of time. One day though, I may need to know how to do this stuff, so now is probably the best time to learn.

Today, I decided to be positive and learn how it's all done. Plus, it will give me a chance to use all the SKILLS I learned from Dad about cooking. His way of cooking is easier than Mom's. Mom does most of the cooking. When she cooks, there's a whole lot going on.

She's got three or four pots on the stove. She's got stuff in the oven, and she's cleaning up too. I can't do all that.

Dad's way of cooking is much easier. He'll only have one thing on the stove, and he uses the microwave oven a lot. And he doesn't worry about making a big mess either.

I remember him telling Mom that the mess he makes in the kitchen makes the food taste better. When I used Dad's cooking technique in class, everybody looked confused.

That home economics class is still NOT my favorite class. When the bell rang to change classes, I was the first one out the door.
On the way to my next class, I saw this really CUTE girl.

She was talking with two other girls and I'm pretty sure she was looking right at me. Then the cute girl said something that made them all laugh. I hope they weren't laughing at me, but if they were, I don't care. At least I don't have a WEIRD sounding laugh like that cute girl's two friends.

They both sounded kind of goofy. I don't understand why such a cute girl would have friends that go "HEE HAW" when they laugh. This could have turned out to be a miserable school day, but seeing that cute girl saved it.

Mom and Dad were shocked when I came in the house excited about school. I think they were hoping I was excited because I learned something new. When I told them it was because I saw a cute girl, they lost interest pretty quickly. Maybe I should have said something like, "I learned that nine is the square root of eighty-one." That would have made them happy for sure.... WOW! I just sounded smart**!!**

Tuesday, September 17th

I got this bright idea when I woke up this morning.

It was to ask Janet about that cute girl I saw yesterday. I would have asked her this morning, but she didn't stop by my house to pick me up. I figured something was wrong, so

I stopped by her house on the way to school. Her Mom answered the door and said that Janet had a bad cold and was staying home from school. That meant I'd have to wait until tomorrow to ask her about the cute girl. What a ROTTEN day to get sick and stay home from school. I don't mean to sound like an uncaring JERK.

I DO care that she's sick and has a bad cold. She just picked a rotten day for it. Okay, I'm not just a jerk, I'm an out-of-control jerk.

When I got to school this morning, Dino was standing outside waiting for me.

I knew his Mom was transferring him to my
school, but I didn't know when. As soon as his
Mom drove off, he started in with a million
questions. "Where are the lockers? What are
they serving for lunch today? How do I find my
homeroom?"

I didn't have time to answer all of his questions
or show him the whole school. I was already
LATE for class. So, I brought him inside and
pointed to the first door I saw with a knob on it,
and told him that's where he needed to go.

It turned out to be the broom closet. But I knew he could figure out how to get around.

He could ask his teacher or one of the kids in his class. Who knows, he might even run into the super smart kid with the big head like I did.

At lunchtime, I was already in the cafeteria when I saw Dino walk in. I called him over to sit with Mia, Kelly and me. As soon as the girls saw Dino, I thought, "uh-oh! Dino might become the girls' next victim!" They're probably thinking "Why did he wear those clothes, look at his hair, listen to the WAY he talks." They'll pick him apart. I was worried. But amazingly, that didn't happen.

They were actually NICE to him. Even when he got up to get his lunch, they didn't say one mean thing about him behind his back.

They even laughed at his corny jokes. It didn't end there. When the girls started trash-talking the kids in the lunchroom, Dino had this puzzled look on his face, like he didn't know what they were doing.

But then instead of staying quiet like I was, he joined in with them. I couldn't watch that happen.

This was Dino's first day of school. He didn't know any of the kids he was talking bad about. But it didn't matter. Anytime they said something bad about somebody, Dino agreed. It was tough to watch.

At first, I was worried that Mia and Kelly wouldn't like Dino. Now, I'm worried that they like him MORE than they like me.

Wednesday, September 18th

Janet stayed home from school again today. That's two days in a row. I wish she'd come back. I need to find out the cute girl's name. I wasn't going to tell Dino about the cute girl unless it was totally necessary, but now I need his help. Janet may not ever come back to school.

HOW DO I FIND OUT THE CUTE GIRL'S NAME?

WHY NOT ASK HER YOURSELF? WHAT...ARE YA CHICKEN?

Getting Dino involved was a BIG mistake. I was just about to tell him that too when some big guy showed up and got in the middle of everything.

The big guy pulled us apart and said we need to be calm like water, and in harmony with the universe. He said he was practicing to become a monk, and that monks are peaceful.

Me and Dino were both about to start arguing again. Then, he said something that made me think that we really **NEED** to listen to this guy.

That last thing he said didn't sound like "peaceful monk talk" to me, but it got our attention. After that guy left, Dino was still trying to convince me that I should talk to the cute girl myself. I didn't tell him, but he's right. I am going to talk to her myself.

The only thing I'm worried about is if he finds out I used his idea, he'll think he's smarter than me. That'll open up a whole new can of worms.

Thursday, September 19th

Today was the day I was supposed to talk to the cute girl myself. But I chickened out. It was way too scary. I'm going back to my original idea of having Janet talk to her for me. Besides, it was DINO'S idea that I talk to the cute girl myself. And if it was his idea, it COULD'NT be a good one. Mia and Kelly told me at lunch that Janet was supposed to come back to school tomorrow. I wanted to hear that for myself, so on the way home I stopped by her house.

I didn't want to talk to her too much today; I can wait until tomorrow. Plus, she still looks a little sick. If I hang around her too long, I could catch whatever she's got. Okay, I know what you're thinking, and you right, I'm a J-E-R-K!

Later on, I rode my bike to Dino's house. He was already out on his bike trying to do bike tricks. I used to think he was the worst bicycle rider ever. He's NOT the worst ever, but he is a little clumsy. I'm kind of clumsy too, but I don't fall off things half as much as Dino does his bike. The last time I fell off anything was when I was little. I was playing with my toy airplane on the top bunk bed. The plane flew off the bed, and I did too.

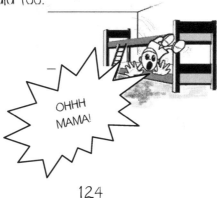

OHHH MAMA!

That was a painful day. Mom and Dad were a little upset. They had to put off our vacation for a week until I felt better.

Friday, September 20th

Today, Janet was back in school. Her Mom drove her in so she wouldn't have to walk. She wasn't in school ten minutes before I started peppering her with questions about the cute girl.

I was doing a lousy job describing the girl to her, and Janet knew it. So, she started asking me questions about the girl. "How long is her hair? What color is it? Is she tall or short?" That was working a whole lot better, but it was still taking her a long time to come up with a name.

I couldn't think of much more to tell her about the girl I saw in the hallway. It looked like Janet was trying to think of every girl she knew in school to come up with the right one.

Janet, Mia and Kelly always have little names they call people. I was kind of worried that if she does know who the girl is, she might not know her REAL name.

I was getting a little frustrated. And I was just about to give up. But then she asked me where I saw her last. "Across the hall from my seventh-period class." I said. That did it. FINALLY, she figured out who it was. I knew she could do it. She said she'd tell her about me tomorrow morning.

Thursday, September 26th

It's been a week and Janet hasn't told the cute girl about me yet. I don't know what to do. Every morning on our way to school, I'll ask her if she talked to the cute girl for me. And every morning she says, "Oh, I'll talk to her today." But she NEVER does. I've decided that every time I see Janet, I'm going to talk about the CUTE GIRL and ask about the CUTE GIRL until it drives her crazy. Or until she actually talks to her for me.

So today, as soon as my first class ended, I ran over to Janet's classroom and waited for her. She was one of the last kids to come out. When she got close enough, I said, "Hey, Janet. Did you talk to the CUTE GIRL for me yet?" She didn't answer, so I kept it going. "When am

I going to meet the CUTE GIRL? Was the CUTE GIRL surprised that I wanted to meet her? Why is it taking so long for me to meet the CUTE GIRL?!" I might have overdone it a bit because she kind of blew a gasket.

Geez, I didn't think she'd freak out like that, but at least NOW I know the cute girl's name. It took a minute or two for her to calm down. Then she told me not to worry; she'd talk to

MARLENE about me today. She NEVER told me not to worry before. This time I actually believe she's going to talk to her. Then I thought about Marlene's friends. Those two girls that were in the hall with her making those "hee haw" sounds. I didn't want her saying anything in front of them.

Maybe I shouldn't have said "GOOFY" friends to Janet. I'm sure she'll do the right thing; she's a good friend. She won't repeat what I said to Marlene. Besides, if she told Marlene I said that, I would have no choice but to put her on my WORST friends list. I don't even have a worst friends list, but if she told her what I said, I'd MAKE one just to put HER on it.

A couple of hours later, I saw Janet in the hall talking to Marlene. When I walked by they both waved to me. I can't wait to tell Dino what a STOOGE he is for giving me that advice.

Telling me I should talk to Marlene myself. Janet and Marlene are friends. It's better if Janet talks to her for me. Tomorrow she should be introducing Marlene to me so I can finally meet her myself. Janet's the best. She's the BEST FRIEND EVER!

Friday, September 27

Janet's the WORST FRIEND EVER! She told Marlene I called her friends GOOFY.

I should have known when Janet told me not to worry, something BAD would happen. Now, thanks to Janet, Marlene hates my guts.

After school, I walked straight over to Janet's house to find out WHY she would ruin my chances with Marlene like that. She must secretly not like me. Why else would she do that?

Janet thinks it's funny, but nobody else does. Especially not Marlene. I hate to say it, but Dino was right. I should have talked to the cute girl myself. I'm making a "worst friend in the world" list. Janet's the only name on it.

Monday, September 30th

Something incredible happened today.
Somehow, it got around the school that I called Marlene's friends goofy.

The kids at school thought that was a RAD thing to do. I've been getting high-fives and pats on the back from some of the coolest kids in school. Some of those kids were telling me she's "popular" and NOBODY has ever talked to her that way before.

I wanted to set them straight and tell them what really happened, but all that attention felt kind of good.

The more people crowded around me, the more JUNK I came up with to tell them.

I said, "I didn't just call Marlene's friends goofy, I called everybody goofy.

Marlene. Janet, all of Marlene's friends, EVERYBODY." They loved it. And now, because they think I said all that stuff, I just became the MOST popular kid in school!

I showed up at school today and people were treating me like a ROCKSTAR. Girls were trying to carry my books, other kids wanted my autograph, and EVERYBODY wants to talk to me. But I'm not letting it go to my head. Well, maybe a little.

If things get any crazier, I'll have to get an ASSISTANT to organize my schedule for me. Kids are inviting me to their birthday parties, and they want me to hang-out with them after school. They're even fighting over me to sit with them at lunch.

Today at lunch, I sat with Tony Rippen. He's a pro level video game player.

Which makes him cool. He said if I sit with him and his friends, I'll make them look even cooler, so I did.

I told them I wanted Dino to sit with us, too. He may never get a chance like this again. Some kids even want to hang out with Dino just because he knows me.

They should make ME in charge of the whole school, but that "principal guy" thinks he's in charge of everything.

I'm having a great time in school, but I'm starting to get the feeling Dino's not very happy about it.

He's my best friend and all, but he needs to be a little more enthusiastic about my new-found popularity.

Just when I'm feeling good about my new situation at school, along comes Janet and Marlene to try and ruin things for me.

First it was just Marlene, and now Janet's mad at me, too. Kids started calling her goofy along with Marlene. Maybe she deserves it. If she hadn't told Marlene what I said about her friends, none of this would have happened.

Janet and Marlene wanted an apology, but I didn't want to do it. I'm a popular kid now. I'm pretty sure popular kids aren't supposed to apologize.

I guess all that "popular-kid" stuff made me a little big headed. They wanted an apology. So, I apologized.

But that wasn't enough. They want me to tell the whole school that I'm sorry for what I said about them. How am I supposed to do that? Get on the school's PA system?

I wouldn't even know what to say. I'll tell you one thing, I would disguise my voice so no one would know it was me. Apologizing could ruin everything.

No Way, I can't do that. If those school kids
find out I DIDN'T say all that stuff about
Marlene and Janet, I'll go back to being a NOT
so popular kid again. No more high-fives, no
more sitting with other popular kids at lunch, no
more pats on the backs. It'll all be over. It's
GREAT being a popular kid. If I knew it was
going to be this good, I would have insulted my
friends a long time ago.

Wednesday, October 2nd

I tried to stay away from Janet all day at school.
I even had to wake up extra early this morning
and leave the house before she came over to
pick me up.

After school, I walked over to Dino's house so
we could figure out how to get ME out of this
mess. He thought I was being a jerk to him too,
so I had to give him an apology before he would
help me. Geez, I've only been popular for a
couple of days. I've spent half that time
apologizing to people.

All I needed from Dino was a way to get the
kids at school to STOP calling the girls goofy.
That wasn't so easy to do, and the ideas he was
coming up with were horrible.

We weren't coming up with anything, and then I got an idea. We could write a NOTE and hang it in the hallway at school. It could say that Marlene and Janet are *COOL.*

Once people read that, they'll stop calling them goofy. The best thing about the idea was that nobody will know I wrote it. I won't have to apologize, and I could continue being the most popular guy in school. Dino added something GREAT to the note. Instead of saying they're cool say, "COOLFY." They're not goofy; they're

coolfy. Finally, he had a good idea. I was
excited. The note was going up tomorrow.

TO ALL SCHOOL KIDS!!
MARLENE & JANET
ARE NOT GOOFY.
IF ANYTHING, THEY'RE
COOL-FY!

Thursday, October 3rd

Hanging the note wasn't easy. We had to put it
up and make a run for it before anybody saw
us. We hid around the corner and saw kids'
reading the note. The plan was working.

Later on, I saw Marlene and Janet. I thought maybe they didn't read the note, because they were still mad at me.

They were trying to tell me kids are still making
fun of them. I told them that was impossible.

Okay, so kids are calling them Coolfy. What's
wrong with that? Coolfy is not even a REAL word.
I don't see the problem with it.

If they called me coolfy, I'd say thanks. Maybe
they don't like it because coolfy sounds too much
like Goofy. Who knows?

Wednesday, October 9th

It took almost a week, but Marlene is finally over the whole COOLFY name calling thing. She's even talking to me now. We've become good friends.

I can't say I'm good friends with the rest of the kids at school though. They're fickle. My popularity didn't last long at all. I'm NOT getting that special "popular-kid" treatment anymore.

It must have been that stupid NOTE we put up in the hallway. I am NOT going back to sitting with Janet and her two friends at lunch anymore. If I have to, I'll stop eating lunch.

Thursday, October 10th

After school, I rode my bike over to Eddie's house, then we rode over to Dino's. He wanted to go bike riding, but not too far away from his house. Which meant riding up and down his

dead-end street. After twenty minutes of that,
I was bored.

I didn't think Dino would follow us, but he did. On
our way back, we passed Mr. Norton's house
with his crazy dog. The dog saw us through the
gate and came running out of the yard barking
his head off. Dino got scared and tried to get
away. The dog saw that and went after him.
I thought Dino would panic and crash into
something, but he didn't. He did a good job NOT
letting the dog catch him.

We wanted to help by racing after him trying to catch up. He was so far ahead we couldn't, but we could see that Dino was heading straight for a big bush. I yelled, "Look out, big bush!" He was so far away, I don't think he heard me, but it didn't matter. With the dog right behind him at the last second, he squeezed his hand brake. The bike STOPPED just SHORT of crashing into the bush. The DOG saw Dino stop but couldn't stop himself, and ran straight into the bush.

It was kind of funny. Dino said to the dog, "What, you don't have hand brakes?" He might have hurt the dog's feelings. He looked at us, growled, and walked away. He really looked upset.

Dino was happy his bike stopped the way it did. His hand brakes made him stop just short of crashing into that bush. Those brakes are awesome! I really wish Mom and Dad bought me the bike with hand brakes. I wish I knew why parents don't always listen to kids.

Friday, October 11th

Halloween is in a few weeks. It's one of my favorite holidays. I can't wait to go trick-or-treating. The only problem is, I've never been trick-or-treating in this neighborhood before. I don't know what to expect. So, I had Dino and Eddie come to my house for a special Halloween strategy meeting.

The great thing about Halloween is you don't have to do anything special to have people just hand you candy. Showing up at their door with a costume is about the hardest thing you have to do. I've seen kids NOT get treats and "TP" a house something awful. That's when wearing a mask and costume as a disguise really comes in handy. Last year on Halloween, me, my old best friend Devin, and this kid Charles Dremer went to the Trippington house. They always went berserk making their house look great for Halloween.

156

They had everything. Scarecrows, skeletons, black bats, all kinds of creepy stuff. We would stop by that house every year. Last year, they even had a mummy sitting by the door that came to life when you rang the bell.

We would have run all the way home if the mummy didn't start laughing. The person in the mummy suit turned out to be Mr. Trippington. Then Mrs.Trippington came out and gave us a LOAD of candy. I think she felt bad that Mr. Trippington scared us the way he did. We were just about to go to our next house when we

saw Big Burt Simmons, the biggest kid in
seventh grade, on his way to the Trippington's
house. We knew if the mummy tried to scare
Big Burt, that might be something you didn't
want to miss. So, we pretended to leave, and
then hid in the bushes next door. When Burt
rang the doorbell, the Mummy said "BOOO!!!"
BIG Burt did what he's famous in school for.

The mummy went down like a sack of potatoes.
Once Burt found out the mummy was Mr.
Trippington, he apologized big time.

Mrs. Trippington saw what happened, and came outside to help her husband back in the house. Then she came back out and gave Burt a load of candy, too.

That's one thing that was great about my old neighborhood. Everybody was so nice. You'll still get lots of candy, even when you PUNCH them in the stomach.

Monday, October 14th

Every year I have to come up with a new costume to wear, but this year I won't have to. Mom told me one of the neighbors has a business making Halloween costumes. She wants to give both Ben and me one.

At first, I was a little worried about that until Mom said that we were getting BASEBALL costumes. That made me feel better. I just hope I get a popular player's costume. Someone that hits a lot of homeruns or something.

Tuesday, October 15th

Turns out when Mom said we were getting BASEBALL costumes she wasn't kidding. I put the costume on, and then called Dino so he could see how ridiculous I looked.

Anytime I don't pick out my own costume, I pay for it. Mom knew I wouldn't want to be a "BALL" for Halloween, but she wanted to see what I looked like in it anyway. I made sure I took it off fast before she went and got her camera. Mom had one for Ben, too. He didn't like his, either.

Thursday, October 17th

Starr got her driver's permit today. And when she found out I had to go to the store to get a NEW costume for Halloween, she begged Dad to let her drive me.

I would have been nervous about her driving us, but Dad was nervous enough for the both of us.

The store was only ten minutes away, but it felt like it took us forever to get there. Being in the car while Starr is driving is fun, but scary at the same time.

She drives too close to the other cars, and way too fast. We made a turn down one street so fast, it felt like we were on two wheels.

Teaching her how to drive is going to be a tough job. When we got to the store, I rushed inside and grabbed the last Constructo Man costume they had left.

I was so HAPPY to get it, I almost forgot Starr had to drive us back home.

Friday, October 18th

Starr getting her learner's permit was the
WORST thing that could have happened to
Dad.

I think he's finding stuff around the house to do,
just so he doesn't have to take her out driving.
And when he does take her out, and they
manage to make it home safe, she wants to go
right back out there again.

I can't blame Dad for not wanting to go. He's so happy he made it back in one piece, why would he want to put himself through that again? Starr now says that Dad doesn't take her out driving enough. So, she wants to BUY her own car, and she wants me to help her.

I don't know why I said MONKEY— it just came out. I don't think she believed me anyway. She got upset, and told me she didn't want my money, and that she'd earn it herself. I DIDN'T know what that meant until later.

165

Starr's trying to charge for everything.
She told me she had a message from Mom but
I had to give her twenty-five cents to find out
what it was.

She even tried charging Mom and Dad for stuff.
Once that didn't work, she started looking
everywhere for money.

If this is the way she plans on getting money for a car, by the time she gets enough, she'll be too old to drive.

Thursday, October 31ˢᵗ

Today is Halloween. Ben tells me Mom wants to take us both trick-or-treating. I told him NO WAY. The last time I went trick-or-treating with Ben, it was a disaster. Any house decorated with a witch or a ghost was too scary for him, so Mom passed the house by.

We only stopped at ten houses the whole night.
I said to him, "I'm going with my friends. I get a
lot more candy that way." Once he heard "more
candy" he ran out of the room.

I told Mom I was planning on going with my
friends, and she was okay with that. Mom told
Ben he had to go trick-or-treating with her, or
he couldn't go at all. He wasn't too happy
hearing that. Right after I put on my Constructo
Man costume. Eddie came by with his costume.

Asking him that question was a big mistake. When you ask the question "Who are you?" to a guy dressed as a clock, you get what you deserve.

As soon as I saw the costume, I should have known he was Tick Tock the Destroyer. That's exactly what the guy in the video game does. I JUST wish he wouldn't do it to my room. Dino called about ten minutes later, wanting us to meet him in front of his house. I had to sneak out of my house and not let Ben see me leave. Knowing Ben, he'd cause such a ruckus that Mom might change her mind and ask me to take him with me. That would ruin everybody's night. Dino was already outside when we got to his house. His costume looked VERY familiar.

I couldn't believe it. He made FUN of me for wearing that costume, then when I wouldn't wear it, he asked my Mom if he could. Maybe he LIKED the costume the whole time. He was right about one thing, that costume does make you look like a FOOL. The GUYS thought I was wasting time with the Halloween strategy meeting, but it turned out to be a good idea. We got candy from most of the houses we stopped at. Dino wanted to go to one more house before going home. He said it was the best Halloween house ever; it looked boring to me.

No lights, no decorations, nothing.

We walked up the path to the house and rang the bell. The door opened, and this lady was standing there with no costume and no candy, but she wanted us to come inside. I looked at Dino thinking, this is the best Halloween house ever? Dino had a big smile on his face and walked inside. We followed him inside and sat on the couch. The lady said she was out of candy, but gave us a handful of loose change.

I still couldn't understand why Dino thought it was such a great place. They didn't even have any candy left, just a bunch of nickels and dimes. We got up to leave when we heard this creepy voice say, "We were having fun with you, Hap-py Hal-lo-weeeen!"

Then this music started playing, the room got dark, all kinds of stuff like skeletons, mummies and black bats dropped from the ceiling.

I told Dino that me and Eddie were getting out of there. He said, "I'm staying. I'm having fun!" Then this witch, flying around on a broom said, "LEAVE NOW!"

I thought that was the best idea I'd heard all night. Eddie was already heading toward the front door, and I was right behind him.
We were just about to run out when the door closed shut. We turned and headed towards an open window, and that closed shut, too.

Me and Eddie ran to the kitchen, opened the door to the backyard, and ran out of there screaming our heads off. We ran all the way around the house to the front yard and down the street, then realized we'd left Dino inside the house.

We were both too afraid to go back and get him. We didn't know what to do. So, we decided to flip a coin. Heads, go back and get him, tails, leave him there and go home. It came up tails.

Flipping the coin was a great idea. He could never blame us for leaving him. We can always say, "We had to leave you— it came up tails." The weird thing was when we got back to MY house, Dino was sitting on the stoop. He said those people at that house do the same thing every year, and that's why he wasn't scared.

He laughed at us for running away like we did, and he laughed some more when he found out Eddie and me lost our bags of Halloween candy. After we stopped feeling bad for ourselves, we realized Dino lost something, too.

Saturday, November 2nd

Ben asked Mom and Dad for a new bike. I guess because I have a new bike, he wants one too. It's not even his birthday. One thing I know for sure, they don't want to get him the wrong bike like they got me. Ben takes full advantage of being the "baby" of the family. If they get him a bike he doesn't want, he'll freak out! Like the time he got the wrong flavored ice cream.

And that was just ice cream. If they get him the wrong BICYCLE, he might take his tantrum to a whole new level. They used to let ME get away with kicking, screaming and rolling around too— not anymore. But that doesn't stop me from trying.

If acting like a baby still worked for me, I could have thrown myself on the floor and gotten the bike I wanted with the HAND BRAKES. I do have it better than Starr, though.

Because she's the oldest, her days of kicking and screaming for stuff are LONG gone. That's probably why she's always so grumpy. She's still holding a grudge over those SMELLY socks I threw at her months ago.

I know because she wrote it down in her diary. She also wrote, "Soon I will strike back and get my revenge." That's why I have to continue READING her diary. If I don't, I'll never know what's going on in her head.
I'm only reading it now for my own safety.

Something else I found out. She's supposed to wake up early tomorrow morning, sneak into my room, and ambush me with a water balloon.

My counter offensive is to wake up even
EARLIER, and leave the house before she
gets a chance to soak me.

Sunday, November 3rd

She'd waited two months thinking I'd forget so
she could get back at me. But it's just like they
say, "You have to wake up pretty early to fool
me— once, and, shame on you if you fool me

two times...?" That's not the saying, but it's something like that. I'm just glad I got up early. It's a good thing Dino wakes up early too, because I had to go to his house until it was safe to go back home. And it wasn't safe until Mom and Dad woke up.

Monday, November 4th

Eddie called me today. He wanted me to stop by his house to check out a new video game he just got called Raving Ranger. He wanted to call Dino too, but I had to remind him that Dino can't play video games on school days. I don't know how Eddie does it. This game was sold out the same day they released it. Nobody can get it, and HE has it. I asked him how he

always manages to get the newest video games. Turns out he's one of those people that will camp out all night waiting for the store to open in the morning. Most times his Mom will camp out at the store for him, especially if he has school the next morning. That's a lot of effort for a video game.

Because I won't camp out, I will never be the first kid on the block with the newest game. I can't sleep outside a video store all night waiting for the store to open, but Mom can. When I asked her about staying out all night in front of a video game store until it opens in the morning, she said that was a DUMB thing to ask her to do.

Then she said I should wear this "thinking cap." It might help me get the games I want. So, I tried it.

While Eddie and me where playing the game,
Dino showed up.

183

Dino said, "I told my Mom I was at the library. So I can stay as LONG as I want." I believe when you tell your Mom a BIG fat lie, you don't show up at your FRIEND'S house so they could get into trouble, too. I wanted Dino to go back home. Eddie wanted him to go back home, too. Eddie thought it would be funny if we scare him into leaving. So, Eddie started talking really loud so his Mom, in the kitchen, could hear him.

Dino started hopping around the room telling Eddie to be quiet. Eddie was right. It was funny watching Dino panicking like he was. It stopped being funny when Eddie's Mom came in the room.

As soon as she left the room Dino bolted out of the house. Eddie ran into the kitchen to see if his Mom was on the phone with Dino's Mom and she was, but only to get a recipe. Eddie came back to tell ME what his Mom was doing, and we ran outside to tell Dino.

Dino was already on his bike about to race home. I said "Dino, you're NOT in trouble," but he didn't believe it.

We chased after him yelling "YOU'RE NOT IN TROUBLE!" But he kept going. Instead of going home his usual way, he took the long way to his house.

I think he did that just in case his Mom was looking out the window. If she saw him, she'd think he was coming back from the library. He's bad about telling his Mom the truth, but he's sure good at covering his tracks.

What he did seemed like a good idea. Then I realized taking the long way meant riding past Mr. Norton's house with his crazy dog. The dog saw us ride past his house, and he started barking like crazy. Then he got out from behind the gate, and came after us—again.

Dino was out front, and just like the last time, that crazy dog went after him. Eddie called out to Dino "Find a big bush and do the STOP SHORT, brake thing again!" Dino looked scared, but found a big bush and headed towards it.

The dog was right behind him huffing, puffing, and barking. Then Eddie decided he'd get in on the action, so he RACED to catch up with Dino and the dog. As soon as he got there, Eddie started giving Dino all these DIRECTIONS. "Ride faster. Squeeze the left-hand brake. Slow down a little." Then he said, "When I yell *BRAKE*, squeeze the right-hand brake." I think Dino got confused by all the stuff Eddie was telling him to do. Then Eddie screamed, "BIG BUSH! BRAAAKE!!"

They both squeezed their brakes at the same time and went flying off their bikes and OVER the big bush.

The dog was smart. As soon as Eddie yelled "BRAKE", he stopped running. I guess he remembered crashing into the bush the last time.

He wasn't about to do it again. The dog sat
there and watched them fly over the bush, too.
They both hit the ground pretty hard. I rushed
over to help them up.

That fall really scrambled their brains.
Dino kept asking what happened. I told him he
had squeezed the wrong hand brake, and it
threw him off his bike. I don't think he
understood me. Then, he started counting his
arms, legs and fingers to make sure all of his
body parts were still there. Dino and Eddie
were HURT so bad, they didn't even want to

ride their bikes back home. So, we picked the bikes up off the ground and walked home. As soon as I got in the house and saw Mom, I told her what happened, and I also told her how much I like my PEDAL brake bike.

I guess I wanted a bike like Dino's because I thought it looked COOL, and because my friends had one.

After we talked, I left the room, I KNEW if I stayed around too long, I was going to hear the words, I TOLD YOU SO.

Monday, November 4th

Dino stayed home from school today. He hardly EVER misses school. He thinks if he doesn't go to school, he's missing out on something. Later on, I walked over to his house. I was shocked to see how hurt he was.

I knew he was hurt, but I didn't think he had sprained his ankle. I left Dino's house and stopped by Eddie's. He didn't get hurt at all. He was just angry at THAT dog. He said he and Dino squeezed the wrong brake because the dog TRICKED them.

Eddie said, "As soon as I yelled, BRAKE, the dog STOPPED running. He wasn't supposed to do that." I tried telling him what Mom said about young kids and hand brakes, but he wasn't listening. He was sure the DOG was the problem. He wanted to know how a dog could be so smart.

He thought he needed his OWN dog to understand what happened. So, he asked his Mom if he could have a dog and keep it in his room.

His Mom said YES to the dog, but NO to keeping it in his room. So, he decided to BUILD a dog.

COULD YOU PASS ME THAT HEAD OVER THERE?

I felt like asking Mom if I could keep a dog in my room, but she might think it's a dumb idea, and have me put on that CONE shaped THINKING cap again.

Tuesday, November 5th

Starr never got me back for throwing my smelly socks at her. I know she had to be planning something. So, I read HER diary again to find out. And it's a good thing I did. She wrote, "Today I right a wrong. Months ago, I smelled his stinky sock. Today, it will be the sweet smell of success." I went into the living room to ask Mom if she knew where I could find my red shirt with the big buttons. Then I hear someone say, "There's a lot you don't know." And when I turned around...

She ambushed me. Finally, she got her revenge. One thing she forgot though, Mom put me on punishment for two weeks with

that whole sock thing. So, I hope she doesn't have anything planned for the next two weeks.

For more stories from the Any Kid USA bunch, email us.

Anykidusa@gmail.com

Acknowledgements

I want to start by thanking my soul mate Jeanick Maximilien. I can't count how many times I asked her to reread something right in the middle of her favorite TV show. I do know it was many times, and she never complained. Babe, you're the best!

To my mom, Faridah Omar who passed away in 2011. If she hadn't encouraged me the way she did all through my life, I don't know if I would have been an author today.

To my father Faried Omar Sr. for instilling in me the life lessons which have been my foundation in life. Thank you to Laura Tria, my extraordinary accountability partner. Without her, I wouldn't have been able to continue working on this project for five years.

To my book editor Susan Kiley, thank you for your talent and input. Thank you to my cousin James Vann. He took time out from his busy schedule to create the characters for this book, and he really made my words come alive. Also, to Ronaldo Florendo, a super talented Illustrator. To my sister Zakiya Omar, who gave me a few key suggestions when I so much needed them.

About the Author

Abdul Swift grew up in New York, and as a youth, he and his friends would spend hours drawing the super hero characters he saw in comic books. His love for books and the comics was his motivation to create his own book.

After a few failed attempts, he got the idea to create the first edition in a series of books called Any Kid USA. Abdul Swift is a Certified Self Esteem Coach for children and also a Certified Life Coach.

He has a son and daughter in college, and they live on Long Island, NY.

44744438R00125

Made in the USA
Middletown, DE
10 May 2019